MOUNT PLEASANT

DISCARDED

ME I

AM!

Jack Prelutsky

Pictures by Christine Davenier

Melanie Kroupa Books
Farrar, Straus and Giroux ⬩ New York

Text copyright © 1983 by Jack Prelutsky
Illustrations copyright © 2007 by Christine Davenier
All rights reserved
Distributed in Canada by Douglas & McIntyre Ltd.
Color separations by Chroma Graphics PTE Ltd.
Printed and bound in the United States of America
by Phoenix Color Corporation
Designed by Barbara Grzeslo
This edition, 2007
10 9 8 7 6 5 4

"Me I Am!" originally appeared in *The Random House Book of Poetry for Children*, New York: Random House, 1983. We are grateful to Jack Prelutsky and Random House for granting us permission to use it in this picture book.

www.fsgkidsbooks.com

Library of Congress Cataloging-in-Publication Data
Prelutsky, Jack.
    Me I am! / Jack Prelutsky ; pictures by Christine Davenier.
        p.   cm.
    ISBN-13: 978-0-374-34902-8
    ISBN-10: 0-374-34902-9
    1. Children's poetry, American.   I. Davenier, Christine, ill.
II. Title.

PS3566.R36M4 2007
811'.54—dc22

2005052758

In memory
of
Martha Alexander
—J.P.

To all the ME I AM's
who helped create this book,
with special thanks
to Melanie
—C.D.

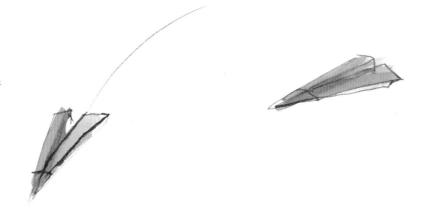

I am the only ME I AM
who qualifies as me;
no ME I AM has been before,
and none will ever be.

No other ME I AM can feel
the feelings I've within;

no other ME I AM can fit
precisely in my skin.

There is no other ME I AM

who thinks the thoughts I do;

the world contains one ME I AM,
there is no room for two.

I am the only ME I AM
who qualifies as me;
no ME I AM has been before,
and none will ever be.

No other ME I AM can feel
the feelings I've within;

no other ME I AM can fit
precisely in my skin.

There is no other ME I AM

who thinks the thoughts I do;

the world contains one ME I AM,
there is no room for two.

I am the only ME I AM
who qualifies as me;
no ME I AM has been before,
and none will ever be.

No other ME I AM can feel   the feelings I've within;

no other ME I AM can fit

precisely in my skin.

There is no other ME I AM
who thinks the thoughts I do;

the world contains one ME I AM,
there is no room for two.

I am the only   I AM
this earth shall ever see;

that ME I AM I always am

is no one else but—

ME I AM!

I am the only ME I AM
who qualifies as me;
no ME I AM has been before,
and none will ever be.

No other ME I AM can feel
the feelings I've within;
no other ME I AM can fit
precisely in my skin.

There is no other ME I AM
who thinks the thoughts I do;
the world contains one ME I AM,
there is no room for two.

I am the only ME I AM
this earth shall ever see;
that ME I AM I always am
is no one else but ME!